THE WORLD ACCORDING TO THE CONFESSIONS OF LASSER VICE
(list Welsh foghorn voice of contradicted coarseness)

THE WORLD ACCORDING TO THE CONFESSIONS OF LASSER VICE

by

d.p. houston

ACCORDING TO THE WORLD CONFESSIONS OF LASSER THE VICE
idiotsavantattainsvoididiotsavantattainsvoididiotsavantattainsvoididiotsavantattainsvoid

This is a Grating Wringer Press Publication

ISBN : 978-1-326-48301-2

The World According To The Confessions Of Lasser Vice
©ulprit : d.p. houston, 2021.

First version printed 2019; a few copies, privately dispersed.

d.p. houston

1985-2021

Lasser Vice

*Metaphors are figures of possession.
Similes are siblings swapping shirts.
Kindred spirits thrive in comparison.
All discover exorcism hurts.*

d.p. houston

Contents

p.4 : *camp out reader*
p.6 : *pulpier enigma*
p.7 : *vet altered self*
p.8 : *a tinny bloodletting*
p.9 : *corny growling*
p.10 : *ex spied six geese*
p.11 : *O, the phoneme*
p.12 : Noblesse oblige
p.13 : *does stargazer lip ethics?*
p.14 : *Blameless Elder Maniac*
p.15 : Shit Midas
p.16 : *popular puritanical rot* [4]
p.17 : *bodkin fuel* ~ Taplow kill ~ *rub a hole via pathogenic verity*
p.18 : *inert profanity*
p.19 : E.G. *rudely germinated*
p.20 : *adman lifts ode's falsest diamond*
p.22 : *incoming tease* ~ Volcano Day doggerel ~ *help yourself*
p.23 : shucks
p.24 : *men seem deadpan* ~ horny cliché's repartee
p.25 : *soul's lurid clef*
p.26 : *her integer seethes*
p.27 : et donc...
p.28 : *Rotten Eyelash (wretch lies therein)*
p.30 : Lasser's *classroom map* ~ fudge agnostic work
p.31 : *I want autopsy* ~ porn collects cum
p.32 : *kooky, we babble*
p.34 : *sire venal pun*
p.35 : *nice beast's epic tune* ~ *l'alchimie d'amour*
p.36 : *desiccate front fig*
p.37 : Modus Vivendi
p.38 : *libel louche ice-men*
p.40 : *boner dowses wall*
p.41 : *repress relit naysayers* ~ happily twin*
p.43 : *sing a maze*

*up with the lark...

Lasser Vice

*the wolf you keep fed
is the one that will win
but beware of the bones
of the beast you keep thin*

(If we take wikipedia's word for it, the original parable's roots are unclear :
either Cherokee folklore or a Billy Graham homily...*asher cans on goo*.)

d.p. houston

Jack of Clubs

What a preposterous inkling it is
to think "something now needs to be said".
(Drake and his pirates descend on Cadiz
and the quayside *hermanos* are dead.)

What a back-buggering burden we bear
when events insist Something Be Done.
(Oswald thanks Ruby for clean underwear
and the bullets fly back to his gun.)

Such an intractable labyrinth spools
that the day's lost and all clues are broken.
(Bristling analysts flock to down tools
and the voices of reason have spoken.)

Lasser Vice

ask me no questions
(UNEASY LIES THE HEAD)

*"Oh heav'nly fool, thy most kiss-worthy face
Anger invests with such a lovely grace,
That Anger's self I needs must kiss again."*
                                       Sir Philip Sidney.

A family man, who adores his dear daughter.
(Collateral damage is thicker than water)

Friend of the Serbs, but their leader's true scourge.
(Business and pleasure explosively merge)

Hard is the key that will pick all our locks.
(Sex with a virgin will cure the pox)

More sorrow than anger propels our chaste fire.
(Numinous robes of the Emperor's choir)

If bombing seems cruel, is apathy kind?
(A hard man may be good to find)

"No new tyrants" - read my lips.
(The Pyrrhic dance? Just move your hips)

Let virtuous necessity be never slandered vice.
(Values are everything - bugger the price)

April, 1999.

d.p. houston

crowning glory

*And now for Freedom's final rule of thumb :
we'll liberate your ass to Kingdom Come...*

Slot a wog for Freedom.
Ragheads bleed the best.
*Thanatos has seldom
been so cravenly caressed.*

Frag the slags with sorrow
while you wear your tears with pride:
*Victory's Tomorrow
sees you better if you cried.*

Tell them it's regrettable
but for the best they die.
Certain goals are gettable
when fire is free to fly.

*Thanatos has always
been so piously profane.
Fuck the ashen priests who pray
so righteously for rain.*

Slot a wog for Freedom.
Ragheads bleed the best.
*Beg a stupid question.
Others take the test.*

Lasser Vice

deep six

A simple stanza for a simple soul
might start something like this : with sounds unseen,
unheard-of sight, the outside in-between.

For complex folk a complex verse would roll
across the page with no more ardent goal
than making clarity appear unclean.

Best complicated purity demean
itself in jest : what price the folderol?

Ex-

egesis was in the beginning.
The footnotes have gone on ahead.
Here's a coda to start the ball spinning,
a cracked floor all dancing-shoes dread.

d.p. houston

*Dalesport**

No, I'd forgotten Dalesport -
heedless late one night
of icy rain the ferry left
as always, dead eyes bright.

The rope missed. No one filled his boots
or caught a crab but waves paced
up and down the empty dockside
that was Dalesport's edge, rock faced

with seaweed, salt and cold,
and shuttered kiosks and arcades,
and grey wet rails and wastebins
ripened for the gulls' dawn raids.

And then as now and always round
the swell of something ending
in a patient sigh, or angry whisper,
absolutely comprehending.

---

* *ekphrasis :* **Adlestrop** *by Edward Thomas*

Lasser Vice

One Legible Boss

In this bleak midwinter,
when the maids are cold,
kindness is a weakness :
harshness best be bold.

Staff morale will splinter
if you don't play fair -
slaps for Jane, smacks for Jill :
Cruelty is Care.

d.p. houston

also sprach der Zeitgeist

I'm sick of being startled.
My mind is overblown.
I need something predictable,
like Midas on his throne.

*As townies by the cart-load
delight in fields unsown,
the straw-man in his fixed abode
makes hay with matches thrown.*

Lasser Vice

*la*BDSM

Signora Fortuna,
my lush lady luck :
from this thicket a rose
for your manicured pluck.

Signora Fortuna,
my sweet muse of chance :
must you stand on my toes
when the dice come to dance?

Signora Fortuna,
my fine bitch on heat :
my readies are willing
to fall at your feet.

Signora Fortuna,
my wanton Gestalt :
will you beef up my shilling
or slug me with salt?

d.p. houston

sadism hit

mojo de merde
je vous en prie
I'm running scared
I cannot see

mojo de merde
excuse my French
but I'm too tired
to dig your trench

mojo de merde
ca va, mon vieux?
I'm ill-prepared
what else is new?

mojo de merde
you've had your time
my luck has spared
her Valentine

mojo de merde
you scratched my back
your trumpets blared
we're in the black

mojo de merde
you've had your fun
I'm running scared
thy will be done…

Lasser Vice

G.M. Food

Hell for Hopkins was
a German butcher : "No **Wurst**,
there is none...**again.**"

aposiopesis

every word counts :
get what you want saying said
even if it's just

Ursula Andress

She frightened the kid
silly - now the daft old goat
knows better, still shakes.

express & admirable

*mea maxima
Tulpa*, a thought-form so fit
I could swive the dream.

Boiled Funk

Porn wants a make-over :
balance the goal.
Eat out my *chakra*
& come in my soul.

Agape's gagging
for lust's divine farce.
Who's up for banging
this fine *caritas?*

Pillow Talk

Predation predates pre-history.
Before-before is when it all began.
The bad seed's root holds no great mystery :
it's deep within the basic heart of man.

keep the faith

Someone somewhere's
up to something :
some will get it, others won't.

Somewhere someone's
down to nothing :
one last chance to stop it.
Don't.

Lasser Vice

Zombie Jesus ate my sins :
I hope he doesn't choke.
*(Hopes, of course, inflame God's grins,
then up they go in smoke.)*

*   *   *

We don't believe in Jesus
& we don't care why he bled.
We believe in compound interest
& reciprocated head.

*   *   *

Orgulous lion
or innocent pup :
the Lord your God will
still fuck your ass up.

d.p. houston

dear Emily

Said Death :
"Sir, please excuse
my clumsy verse,
but I'm so hungry
I could eat a hearse."

dear Gertrude

Roses are roses.
Violets are not.
Flowers with voices
would whisper *"so what?"*

Lasser Vice

a List of Demands

I want your key in my lock
I want your ship in my dock
I want your voice in my head
I want your body in my bed
I want your foot in my door
I want your wreck on my shore
I want your milk in my bowl
I want your fire on my coal
I want your air in my lung
I want your tip on my tongue
I want your third in my fifth
I want your length in my width
I want your wine in my glass
I want your French in my farce
I want your rain in my cloud
I want your face in my crowd
I want your time on my hands
I want your castle on my sands
I want your tune in my song
I want your right in my wrong
I want your bars in my cell
I want your frog in my well
I want your drip in my arm
I want your storm in my calm
I want your stroke in my pool
I want your class in my school
I want your grunt in my groan
I want your marrow in my bone
I want your rules in my game
I want your pride in my shame
I want your hoe in my sod

d.p. houston

I want your faith in my god
I want your cream in my pie
I want your apple in my eye
I want your gas in my tank
I want your money in my bank
I want your wheels on my road
I want your secrets in my code
I want your train on my track
I want your load on my back
I want your Trane in my Monk
I want your beat in my funk
I want your bird in my bush
I want your pull in my push
I want your give in my take
I want your ladder for my snake
I want your cross in my naught
I want your ball in my court
I want your flower in my sun
I want your bullet in my gun
I want your pins in my doll
I want your gangster in my moll
I want your beast in my zoo
I want your old in my new
I want

Lasser Vice

*lines become blurred
when the fish loves the bird
because birds that love fish
make a saltier dish*

*

No wisecracking lava,
no Carry-On peaks :
no fulsome palaver,
when Cupid's prick speaks.

*

Selfishness comes
at a terrible cost.
Sound like a crock of?
Ask *Connie Mendfrost*.

d.p. houston

awe

I think the only fit reply
to your sweet, burning gaze
is genuflection.
Don't ask why.
Just let me show you.
Let me blaze a trail
from smitten adoration
to serene desire,
from far-flung rites
to orthodox oration
with the homage of my humble tongue.

It's not just awe that you inspire
when you look at me like that :
you fill my baser core with fire
& make my heart an acrobat.

Lasser Vice

don't ask

I sometimes think it might be nice,
but then I quickly face the facts -
there's no way round this unpaid price :
there's no unscrewing this old vice.

A seldom thought might go like this,
a line determined in its tracks -
too serious to take the piss :
too pursed to puck a patent kiss.

dance class

If ever you give me the chance
I hope I'll still remember
all the moves required
when lovers dance
the horizontal samba.

d.p. houston

Full Disclosure

Tell me what we'd do, we two,
if we were joined as one.
In long, explicit detail,
tell me who does what to whom,
and how it's done - if gently,
quite how slow - if greedily,
how rough - and tell me how
we'll never have enough of one
another's pleasure, scent, and skin,
how we'll be bound so close
that neither of us knows ex-
actly where our limits end,
nor where the other's may begin.

All this allow, and in return
my tongue shall play its part.
We'll parse the lines, for time's to burn :
just promise not to fart.

Lasser Vice

ye shall not eat of it, neither shall ye touch it, lest ye die...

Feed me the fruit of the Bullshit Tree
that flourishes across the sea.
Lay me out beneath her limbs
where I can offer loving hymns.

Pamper me with Bullshit Oils,
that secret scent when love uncoils.
Slick my body, legs and arms.
Soothe all fear, dissolve all qualms.

Heat my skin with Bullshit Sun :
warm, then hot, til juices run.
*(Lovers' sweat together blended,
passion proved with flesh distended.)*

Carry me to Bullshit Land
& lay me down upon the sand.
Hold me gently. Hold me fast.
Promise me this dream will last.

d.p. houston

so there...

You came. You saw. You balked.
I listened while you talked
& wondered who the hell
you were. We might as well
declare the matter closed.
Its questions can stay posed
for all I care. Just don't
ask me for more. I won't
have anything to say.
Some people get that way
when they've been taken for
a ride. You've left me raw.
Pluck someone else to fuck
around. I wish you luck.
You'll need it. Fools like me
are hard to find. You'll see.

l'esprit d'escalier's lips got there first : bonniest *mots* are the ones you've rehearsed.

Lasser Vice

we like short shorts

    The Queen has been
      a great success.
    (And the Soviet Union
      wasn't a mess.)

                              When Charles[3]
                                  gets the bird
                            will the King due in next
                            be delighted or vexed?

    I imagine Prince Philip
      is hung like a whip :
        long and thin
      and mean as sin.

                                Good Queen Edward :
                                  no such thing.
                            But what sharp joy
                            such news would bring.

    Princess Anne
      is not a man.
    Nor, of course,
      is she a horse.

                                The Duke of York
                                turned pale as chalk :
                                  it seemed his ex
                                    liked pedal sex.

d.p. houston

                Princess Margaret :
                    easy target.
                 Booze and fags
                 & bags of shags.

Hirohito
(unlike Tito)
was never the object of Evelyn Waugh's rants
about the contents of his pants.

                               Cliff Richard :
                                hardly hard.
                                Is this why
                             he looks so spry?

Mister Blobby
had a sordid hobby.
What went on between him and his beagle
was, to say the least, illegal.

                               Bill Wyman :
                               top fur-pie man.
                               Too bloody randy
                               to keep his hands off Mandy.

Served a Big Mac
 Jacques Chirac
let his cutlery loll :
"Cette vache-ci, c'était folle?"

                               George Carey
                               & the Virgin Mary
                               had one hell of a schism
                               on heterosexual proctotropism.

Lasser finds a Moral Compass

We are the Humpers of Moralk,
and you are about to be fucked :
nothing you can't take we'll balk at,
and all of your oysters we'll shuck.

*You are the Humpers of Moralk
and we are about to get punked.
All of this tiresome small-talk
reminds us our time is defunct.*

on Oath

swearing's Big
& swearing's clever :
these days more
than fucking ever.

d.p. houston

Ballad of a Lonely Swordsman

Lasser Vice don't fuck for nothing.
Lasser Vice don't come for free.
If you think his dick is something,
   you should see his salary.

Lasser Vice has depths (most hidden.)
We should prize his mystery.
Garnets twinkle in the midden.
Lasser Vice n'est pas compris.

PC Muscle Control

The wise man remembers
these lost words of Hegel :
you want a tight tuchus?
So do your damn Kegels.

Woke Bloke, Baby

He's a Woke Bloke, baby,
don't even ask :
amenable to every task.

The Woke Bloke, baby, keen to sup
the soya milk filling his recycled cup.

Woke Bloke, baby : have a word.
It's hard to tell which one's the bird.

Woke Bloke, baby : it's perfectly plain.
He'll know he's at fault if you ever complain.

Woke Bloke, baby : give me strength.
He'll slip you a reluctant length
(but only when, to keep things fair,
you've pegged him like you just don't care.)

Woke Bloke, baby, knows his place :
eager to please when you cushion his face.

Woke Bloke, baby, knows the score :
birthday head but nothing more.

Woke Bloke, baby : do your worst.
Squeeze his bollocks til they burst.

d.p. houston

Woke Bloke, baby : what a blurt.
Boot him til your tootsies hurt.

Woke Bloke, baby : let him bask
in the rays that emerge
from the sun in your arse.

Woke Bloke, baby : *oh là là*.
Scoff your shit like caviare.

Woke Bloke, baby : you're so fine.
Necks your piss like vintage wine.

Woke Bloke, baby : on the rise -
servitude his certain prize.

Woke Bloke, baby :
and when you turn blue,
he'll know how you feel
coz he's ragging it too.

Praline Venus

Whack it all on Zero.
Flush it down the pan.
Be a fucking hero,
like the Gambling Man.

Finger in the socket,
always knows the score.
Fuck-all in his pocket :
Lady Luck's a whore.

Nothing left to hazard,
no cards left to turn.
Onward to the scrap-yard :
let the bridges burn.

Spunk it all on Zero.
Splash it down the drain.
What a fucking hero,
sticking dust on rain.

d.p. houston

concrete proof
ceci n'est pas une bite

X.x.X
(sec)
(sec)
(sec)
(sec)
(sec)
(sec)
(sec)
(sec)
(sec)
(sec)
(sec)
(((sac)))
((((sac))))
(((((sac)))))
((((sac))))
(((**secs**)))

....
....

As from thy piss the sweetest lemonade,
so from these farts a fine fanfaronnade...

Lasser Vice

Speak Up, Lad

(Yorkshire traditional bawdy)

A fat lass
in a leather skirt
sat on his face.
Her name was Bert.

She soaked his tonsils
when she came :
his voice has never
been the same.

She hosed him once,
she hosed him twice :
his vocal chords
have paid the price.

Now every time
he tries to talk
all he can do
is fucking squawk.

d.p. houston

Void Vein's Mud

No reading on the shitter.
Stay the fuck away from brass.
Don't get to 40 bitter :
try to have a bit of class.

Feast when you're weary,
and sleep when you're hank.
Wash when you're horny,
and fuck when you're rank.

If you do as I preach,
you'll be ready to land.
If you choose your own beach,
you can count your own sand.

Lasser Vice

all around the World, baby…

((Lasser courting Polly Glott))

In Riyadh, you're my *cariad*.
In Darwin, you're my darlin'.
In *Potsdamer Platz, du bist mein Schatz*.
In Roma, *cara mia*.
In Ho Chi Minh City, you're my kitty.
And Blighty? Aphrodite.
In Panama, you are my star.
In Hobart, you're my sweetheart.
In Darmstadt, you're my pussycat.
More Britain? My sweet kitten.
In *München*, you're my *Kätzchen*.
In São Paulo, *meu anjo*.
In Brasil, you are my greatest thrill.
And here? Different gear.
In Illinois, you bring me joy.
In Maine, it's much the same.
In Alabam', you're my sweet 'dam.
And Florida? *Querida*.
In Kansas, you're my piece of ass.
In Montserrat, *mon chat*.
In Winnipeg, I'll gladly beg :
And Sierra Leone? Ride your new pony!
You drive me crazy in Sulawesi.
In Andorra, I'll adore ya.
In Queensland, will you take my hand?
Malay? I'll say!
In Germany, I kissed your knee.
(In Wales, it never fails.)
In France, we learned a secret dance :
And Greece? Your golden fleece…

d.p. houston

You made me harder in Malta
than the Rock of Gibraltar.
(In Chad you'd never been so bad.)
In Chappaquiddick, you made me thick :
And Burma? Even firmer.
In Adelaide, you're my sweet maid.
In Aberdeen, my Queen.
In Uruguay, you made me sigh.
And Chile? Don't be silly.
In Liechtenstein, you are my wine.
In Libya, my beer.
In New South Wales, I'll taste your ales.
And Egypt? Heaven, sipped.
In Thailand, you were lovely, tanned.
In China, even finer.
In Vietnam, the finest ham :
In Laos, my sugar mouse.
Throughout Kuwait, you make me wait,
but in Peru, you yield anew.
In Israel, I wag my tail :
Mauritius? Quite lubricious!
In the Atlantic, I was frantic,
but in Martinique, we scaled a peak.
En Côte d'Ivoire, je vais te boire.
Ici? Mais oui!

Foreplay is king and queen, valet and maid : pussy purrs only when all debts are paid.

Lasser down below

Lasser Vice is in the basement
beating off the days
codifying his debasement
let us count the ways

Sordid screensplash virtuoso
Tango without Cash
lo-falutin jive slo-motion
Gordon with no Flash

The single-handed tosser's
lobbing smokeless toy grenades :
toothless bloody pointless flosser's
mirror masquerades

If you see him coming
better close your eyes and duck :
block him out with static humming
while he tries his luck

Lasser Vice is in the basement
ticking off the days :
if he finds our hidden casement
everybody pays...

L.S.P.

Bonjour, extase.
Ta gueule, tristesse.
Head full of stars :
to hell with stress.

* * *

Steam all my notebooks,
redact all my mail :
the dirtiest looks
are most certain to fail.

Scorch my virtues,
praise my sins :
this is where
the fun begins*.

---

* *poets breakfast musely and then crap all day*

Lasser Vice

Magazines

Ask Me No Questions : first published by **Hazmat** (**11#2**) in 2009, then by **California Quarterly** in 2017 (**43#1**)

deep six & Exegesis, along with p.4's premature coda *(Metaphors)* were published by **thepotomacjournal.com** (2016, **#18**)

Dalesport : **California Quarterly** (**42#3**)

Signora Fortuna (Blameless…in *Contents*) : **View From Atlantis** (webzine, **Autumn 2018**)

A List of Demands & Awe : **California Quarterly** (**40 #1**)

Lasser Vice

naughty jouster speared head